Someday the Sun Will Shine Again

by
Anne Schraff

Perfection Learning® Corporation
Logan, Iowa 51546

Cover Illustration: Doug Knutson
Cover Design: Deborah Lea Bell
Michael A. Aspengren

For information, contact
Perfection Learning® Corporation
1000 North Second Avenue, P.O. Box 500
Logan, Iowa 51546-1099.
Tel: 1-800-831-4190 • Fax: 1-712-644-2392
Paperback ISBN 0-7891-5088-3
Cover Craft® ISBN 0-7807-9065-0
Printed in the U.S.A.

1 The early morning sun peeked in the window of the farmhouse loft. Josephine Thorpe's drowsy eyes opened. She blinked and realized that this would be her last morning on the family farm. From now on she would be spending her days in the clothing factory. Her aunt Lena had gotten her the factory job. Josephine hadn't met Aunt Lena yet. But since they were family, Aunt Lena had invited Josephine to stay with her. Josephine knew she couldn't stay on the farm any longer.

Aunt Lena operated a three-story boardinghouse in Baldwin, Massachusetts. It was a small mill town outside of Boston. She had convinced Josephine that a lot of young girls in the town brought in good wages as sewing machine operators. Josephine was 14 years old, but she would say she was 15. It was 1873, and the mills didn't like hiring girls under 15 anymore. Massachusetts had been the first state to prohibit the employment of children under 15. She didn't want to break the law. But, Josephine reasoned, she was almost 15.

And she did look older than her age. Girls did it all the time, Aunt Lena had told her.

Josephine crawled out from under her quilt and packed all her belongings in two carpetbags. Her father would be taking her down to the train station. She had made up her mind not to show her true feelings. If Ma were still alive, Josephine thought, she would be weeping to see me go. But she quickly dismissed this thought. Her mother had died four years ago. And in her place was now a stepmother with two small children of her own.

Pa showed no emotion as they rode in the wagon toward the train. Josephine watched the wheels kick up a trail of dust behind them.

When they reached their destination, Pa helped Josephine down from the wagon. He walked stone-faced beside her. But when they reached the train, Pa stopped and looked hard at Josephine. She could tell this was difficult for him. He said, "I'm sorry to see you go, Josie. You know it's not of my doing."

Josephine forced a brave smile to her

lips. She knew that it wasn't Pa's decision. Lillian, her stepmother, had made it clear that it would be better if Josephine moved away and started a new life. She was old enough now, Lillian had said. Besides, the little farm house was cramped since the birth of two babies, one right after the other. When Aunt Lena made the offer to Josephine, it seemed the right thing to do. Josephine didn't feel she had much of a choice.

"Good-bye, Pa. I will write as often as I can," Josephine said as she hurried to board the train. Josephine found her seat and set down her two bags. She looked back through the window to see her father. He held his hat in his hands and looked at the ground. Finally, Pa turned away. He slowly climbed back on the wagon and headed home alone.

Josephine let out a sad and lonely sigh. She wanted to leave the farm but only because she had never gotten along with Lillian. As Josephine grew older, it had gotten worse. She remembered being referred to repeatedly as "lazy and good-for-nothing." Josephine was as tall as a woman. And therefore Lillian thought Josephine should act as an adult and support herself. "Plenty of girls younger than Josephine are out earning wages," Lillian would complain to Pa. Josephine hated even sitting down to eat with the family. She knew that Lillian begrudged her every bite of meat, every biscuit.

As the train rolled east, warm tears spilled down Josephine's cheeks. Now nobody that mattered could see her cry— just the strangers on the train. So she didn't fight the tears. Josephine had not wanted Pa to see her cry. She thought he might tell Lillian. And she didn't want to risk allowing Lillian that satisfaction. After a while, Josephine finally wiped away her tears and stared out the window of the train.

The green expanse of countryside whizzing by her eyes still looked familiar. But Josephine came to realize that she was leaving everything she had ever known. Even the little cemetery where her beloved mother was buried. Since her mother's death, Josephine had visited there every week. She would place flowers that she carefully picked on her mother's grave. Now nobody would do that anymore. Nobody.

Then her thoughts turned to her best friend. Addie Norman had wept bitterly when she had found out that Josephine was leaving. During their last Sunday together, Addie cried, "Oh, Jo, I can't believe that you're leaving. I might never see you again."

"I don't fit in at my house anymore," Josephine had tried to explain. "Ma and me and Pa and my brother, John, we were a family. When Ma died and Lillian came, John went West. Then there was just me. Lillian didn't want that. That's why she and Pa had a new family real soon. She wanted her babies to be the only children in that house. I'm the fifth wheel on the wagon."

"Oh, Jo, you are so brave," Addie raved. Her eyes were wide in admiration. Josephine was the stronger of the two friends. At least outwardly. "I would die if they sent me away all by myself," Addie said.

Josephine had tried to comfort Addie,

and herself. "I won't be all by myself. Aunt Lena, Ma's sister, is there," she said. "I don't know her, though. Aunt Lena and Ma weren't real close. 'Bout once a year they'd send letters, just to keep up with each other. But that was it. I just hope she's someone like Ma."

Josephine had tried to be strong. But now, sitting on the train and watching familiar landscapes fly by, Josephine *was* frightened. She wasn't sure what she was frightened of. Maybe the unknown. Or maybe knowing that her life had changed drastically in the matter of a day. Only yesterday she was riding horses with Addie. They were tumbling in the meadow playing games. Now she had only one reminder left of her childhood.

Josephine reached down for one of her carpetbags and thrust her hand inside. She felt around until she found what she was looking for, near the bottom. She removed the object from the bag. Then she carefully unwrapped the piece of protective calico she had swaddled it in. It was a beautiful doll with a china face and a dress Ma had sewn. At one time it had been lovely. But now it was old and faded. But Josephine didn't care. She held the doll close to her. She wasn't about to leave her doll for Lillian to throw on the fire.

Before Josephine knew it, the train was pulling up to the station at Baldwin. The town was made up of rows of mills on a canal. Before the use of steam had been discovered, water from the canal had powered the cotton mills. Now those mills were filled with sewing machines. They turned out ready-to-wear clothing for men and women. Soon Josephine would sit before one of those machines.

As her eyes scanned the unfamiliar town, she noted how drab and gloomy it looked. She pictured the rolling green farmland of home—this looked far less inviting.

The train rolled to a stop. Josephine gathered her carpetbags and started for the door. She searched the waiting crowd until her gaze met a familiar face, someone who looked like Ma. It had to be Aunt Lena. She was ten years older than Ma would be and many pounds heavier.

But she had the same chestnut hair parted in the middle and drawn back into a bun at the nape of her neck. And she had the same big, wide brown eyes.

"Josephine, is that you?" Aunt Lena called out, waving her arm in the air. "You look about the right age."

"Hello, Aunt Lena," Josephine said after weaving through the gathering of people. "I knew you right away. You look like Ma."

Aunt Lena grimaced. "No. She was the beauty in our family. I was the ugly duckling that never turned into a swan." There was an undercurrent of bitterness in her tone.

Josephine followed Aunt Lena down the street to a three-story brick boardinghouse. Josephine glanced around. All the boardinghouses looked alike. They had all served thousands of working girls from the mills for several decades now.

Josephine followed her aunt into a large front room. Then they climbed up a flight of stairs to a sleeping room. "You'll be sharing your room with another girl," her aunt said.

"That's fine," Josephine said. She thought of the cramped farmhouse. She was used to sharing space.

"Her name is Prudence Kinney, and she works at the mill too. Now, she's older than you and a bit too wise in the ways of the world. You mustn't take to heart everything she says," Aunt Lena cautioned.

Aunt Lena left Josephine to get settled. Josephine sat down on the bed and dropped her bags at her feet. Aunt Lena had informed her that Prudence was still working at the mill and wouldn't be home until about 7:00. Josephine looked around the drab room that she would share. At least it had a window, she noticed.

She crossed the room and looked out at the street. At her bedroom window on the farm, she'd watch the cows coming through the meadow. Here there were no pleasant sights. Only the crowded little mill town and tired people stumbling along like sleepwalkers. And smoke and dirt and the noise of wagon wheels clattering. Now *this* is home, Josephine thought sadly.

At 7:30 Josephine headed downstairs. Aunt Lena had briefed her on the meal schedule. She served three meals a day to the girls who lived there. They took sandwiches with them to the mill for their midday meal. The girls were allowed only a brief time away from the sewing machines to eat. But in the evenings, a hearty meal was served.

As Josephine entered the dining room, a tall, pretty girl approached her. "Hi, I'm Prudence Kinney," she said. "But you can call me Prudie. Can I call you Jo?"

Prudence had long blond braids across the top of her head and pale blue eyes. But there was a deep weariness about her too. She didn't look robust and healthy like Addie and the other farm girls. There were dark circles under Prudie's eyes.

"I've worked at the factory for more than a year now," Prudence continued. "I've even saved a little money."

Josephine sat down to a meal of pot roast and potatoes. Aunt Lena had made apple cobbler for dessert. Josephine didn't say much during supper. She just listened to the other girls visiting and complaining about their day at the factory. Josephine felt an emptiness growing in the pit of her stomach. After supper, Josephine followed Prudence up to their sleeping room.

"Aunt Lena said we have to be up early to have breakfast and get to the mill on time. So I suppose I ought to get to bed," Josephine said.

Prudence laughed. "I ought to go to bed too, but I'm not going to. All day long I work in that miserable factory. I need to have fun sometime. So in the evenings, I splash cold water on my face, and I make myself go out and enjoy life."

Josephine looked at the older girl. "What's there to do around here?"

"Well, tonight there's a concert. Harold Anton is playing the violin and singing some songs," Prudie said. She undid the braids on her head and piled her long hair into a more stylish do. "Who knows what might happen when you go out and mingle with people, Jo," she said.

"I don't feel like going to bed either," Josephine said. It had been a long day, but she was too anxious about the next day to sleep. "Mind if I join you?"

"I'd love it!" Prudence said. "I hate being alone. How about you? Don't you hate being all by yourself?"

"Yes," Josephine said, but it wasn't completely true. Sometimes she enjoyed sitting in a quiet place and reading a book. And there were worse things than being alone. Like being with someone who abhorred you and had to put up with you anyway. Like Lillian.

Josephine always felt like she was in Lillian's way, like dust. Lillian swept and swept, but the dust was always there. So was Josephine.

The sad truth was that there was no longer anyone at the farm whom Josephine wanted to be with. Or who wanted to be with her. Pa was distant and cold lately. Lillian's babies were too young to be company. Since Ma died, the farm had lost its heart for Josephine. So no matter how cold and lonely Baldwin was, it really wasn't any worse than home, she reasoned.

As they walked down the street of the mill town, other young women were walking toward the concert hall too. They were a garrulous group of girls—all chattering away.

"We aren't allowed to talk when we're at the sewing machines, so all the talk is pent up inside us," Prudence explained. "They think if we talk, our work suffers. They drive us like slave masters. So when we get out in the evening, we can't stop talking."

"Where are you from, Prudie?" Josephine asked. She was curious about her new friend.

"New York," Prudence said. "My family has a farm there. I have seven brothers and sisters. My folks were glad when I left. There were too many mouths to feed. Anyway, I hate my father, so I couldn't wait to go."

"I left my father and my stepmother," Josephine said. "I wasn't welcome there anymore."

Prudence smiled, her blue eyes sparkling in spite of their weariness. "We are peas in a pod, Jo. Sometime maybe we can go to Boston and see what it's like there. Maybe we could get a look at how the high-society women live. Someday I'm going to be in high society. I will loll around in the morning and take two hours to decide which dress to wear. I won't rush like mad like I do now. I won't drape some hideous rag around me so I can get to the mill before the bell rings."

Josephine smiled. "I wonder what it's like to be rich," she said.

"I'm going to find out," Prudence said with determination. "For breakfast I'll dine on fried ham and salt fish, and maybe oysters. I'll sip my coffee endlessly. I'll wear an apron over my silk dress so not a spot gets on it," Prudence continued to dream.

"How are you gonna get rich?" Josephine asked.

"Oh, I'm gonna marry a rich man. I'm saving my money and developing my manners so I can be invited to parties where rich people go. Some rich gentleman will cast his eyes on me and think I am the most cultured of young ladies," Prudence said. "I won't breathe a word of my past to him. He'll never know I've worked like a slave in a mill, coughing from the fumes of the oil lamps. Inhaling cotton particles until my lungs ache."

"I heard that when you spend a long time bent over a sewing machine, your back is permanently deformed," Josephine said.

"I'm not working at it long enough for that to happen," Prudence said bitterly. "But it's true. Working at the machines turns a girl into a wretched old crone before her time. Look how pale I am. I used to have rosy cheeks. Now I spend all day inside. No sun. No fresh air. If I want a glow on my cheeks, I have to rub strawberries on them."

When the two girls arrived at the concert hall, they went in and sat down. Soon a handsome young man with long, curly hair appeared on stage with his violin. He played some lovely, but unfamiliar, tunes.

Then he launched into a stirring rendition of sentimental songs from the Civil War. From "Tenting Tonight" to the "Battle Hymn of the Republic." Applause was hearty when he finished. Josephine noticed Prudence clapping with great vigor. Her eyes glowing, she turned to Josephine. "Isn't he wonderful? Such sincerity. Music makes me happy as a lark. If only I could stay here and just listen to the music . . ." she said. "And never return to that stinking mill!"

2 It was still dark in the morning when Prudence roused Josephine. "Hurry, Jo. We need to wash up and eat before we go to work."

Josephine and the other girls from the boardinghouse rushed through their morning chores. Then they gulped down a breakfast of fried potatoes and ham. Josephine quickly swallowed her coffee. Soon she was running down the street with Prudence toward the row of mills.

Josephine entered the room in the mill where she would work. She saw about 50 young women seated before sewing machines. Prudence hurried to her machine as the shop boss, Horace Slattery, approached Josephine. Mr. Slattery was a gruff-looking middle-aged man with small, hard eyes.

"You know how to use a sewing machine, don't you?" he asked Josephine in a harsh voice. He was taking her to her work table as he talked.

"Yes," Josephine said. A Singer sewing machine salesman had come to her town offering classes. Most of the young farm girls and women enrolled. Josephine had learned enough to make simple garments.

"Bertha Paine will show you what to do," Mr. Slattery said. Bertha stood behind Josephine and laid out her work. Bertha was a tall young woman, about 20 years old. She stood over Josephine for most of the morning, explaining how to use the machine for this particular work. Josephine was very nervous and made a lot of mistakes. But Bertha was patient. And by midday, Josephine felt the task was going much more smoothly.

"You'll be able to do the work, Josephine," Bertha assured her. "When I started, I was clumsier than you. And now I'm a supervisor." Bertha left Josephine to sew on her own. She then circled the room checking other girls' work.

The air was bad inside the room. Dust and bits of cotton were always in motion. Ventilation was poor, and the acrid smell from the oil lamps was sickening. It was so dark, even at high noon, that the lamps barely gave enough light to work by. But Josephine tried not to notice anything but the machine before her. And the need to correctly guide the fabric so the seams would be straight and smooth.

"No!" Mr. Slattery shouted into Josephine's ear, startling her. She didn't even know he had been standing there watching her. Now he snatched the shirt she was working on. "It's uneven! You're doing it all wrong. You are stupid. Do you hear me? Stupid! Do it over!" He shook the shirt at her as he yelled.

Josephine was shaking with fear as Bertha hurried over. Josephine wasn't used to being treated this way. Lillian didn't like her, but at least she rarely yelled. She merely ignored Josephine or made snide comments to her. Bertha stood at Josephine's side for another 30 minutes, guiding her.

Mr. Slattery came back to check on Josephine again. "Shoddy work will not be accepted," Mr. Slattery barked. "If you're not clever enough to do it correctly, I can't use you!"

Josephine was so afraid of making more mistakes that she slowed down. Once more Mr. Slattery pounced on her. "You're too slow! You must work faster," the old boor cried.

Josephine worked on, her shoulders aching unmercifully from sitting hunched over the machine for such a long time. When the bell rang signaling the midday meal, she was so stiff she could hardly rise.

Josephine glanced at Prudence across the room. She surveyed the pile of finished work next to Prudence's machine. Then Josephine looked at her own mound of completed projects. Prudence's was stacked impressively high compared to Josephine's. Josephine let out a sigh. But, she reassured herself, Prudence was experienced. And this *was* Josephine's first day.

Josephine ate her cheese and rye sandwich and looked gloomily at Prudence. "Mr. Slattery yelled at me something fierce. I'm so scared I won't keep this job."

"He's a vile man," Prudence said, making a sour face. "He likes scaring girls, 'specially the new ones. I've seen him hit girls for making simple mistakes." Her words didn't make Josephine feel any better.

Josephine hadn't finished eating when the bell rang again. It meant that the girls needed to quickly return to their stations. Josephine shoved the last bite into her mouth and scurried back to her machine.

Josephine noticed Mr. Slattery examining the piles of the girls' finished work. He was walking around the room, inspecting each piece. She dreaded the moment when he reached her pile.

When he finally arrived, Josephine didn't look at him. Instead she tried to concentrate on her sewing. He spent the longest time there, making Josephine extremely nervous. Finally, he threw the garments down and scowled, "Your work is terrible. I warn you, unless you do better quickly, you'll be tossed out in a hurry. Do you understand me?" He shook his finger in Josephine's face as he yelled.

Josephine took a big breath. She mustered the courage to look up at the man. Her voice shook when she answered him. "I'm trying very hard. I know I can learn to be a very good sewing machine operator. Bertha thinks I can manage it," Josephine said.

Mr. Slattery glared at Josephine and snapped, "Damage any of the garments you're working on by your sloppy work, and it will be deducted from your wages."

The other girls, mostly thin and pallid from long hours in the mill, stared at their work as Mr. Slattery yelled at Josephine. They were afraid to look up. The same thing had happened to most of them. By terrifying the new workers, Mr. Slattery thought there was better discipline in the mill.

Mr. Slattery stormed off to tyrannize another girl. And Josephine returned to her work. Her back and shoulders ached more fiercely than before. She was not used to sitting in one position like this. At the farm, Josephine had performed many different chores and had used different muscles. But here she used the same motions over and over. She felt as if a sword were piercing her back and slowly turning.

Josephine felt dizzy as the material moved before her eyes. She feared she'd grow faint and fall into the sewing machine. Mr. Slattery would then descend on her with wild fury and, perhaps, beat her! Josephine had no doubt that it could happen.

When the bell finally rang ending the 12-hour day, Josephine staggered to her feet. Bertha came over and laid a hand on her aching shoulders. "Today was the worst day. Tomorrow will be easier and the day after, better still. Just go home and rest."

"Thank you," Josephine said, walking leadenly towards the door. The fresh night breeze felt good against her face after being shut up in the foul, stagnant air all day. Prudence met up with her as they headed toward the boardinghouse. "Oh, Prudie," Josephine sighed, "I feel like my back is broken! I've never had such a miserable day in all my life." Tears were forming in her eyes.

Prudence shrugged her shoulders and said, "Oh, you'll get used to it, Jo. They say you get used to anything if you're at it long enough."

"I'm terrified of that horrible Mr. Slattery. I think he hates me," Josephine said.

"He hates all of us. He can't imagine

why we can't work like the machines,"
Prudence answered. "He doesn't think
we're human beings. Once I saw him box
a girl's ears 'cause she broke a part on the
machine. The poor girl never heard right
after that. Slattery has a money box where
his heart's supposed to be."

Josephine was afraid that she had made
a terrible mistake in coming to Baldwin.
She should have never left the farm, no
matter how much Lillian despised her.

Aunt Lena herself had worked in a
cotton mill when she was younger. She
had saved her money and bought the
boardinghouse, and now she did well.
Aunt Lena had said she thought Josephine
could handle the work, but she was
wrong. Right now, Josephine was sure she
wouldn't succeed. Her mind raced
desperately to find a way to return to the
farm.

But then Lillian's angry face came to
Josephine's mind. She saw Lillian Thorpe
folding her long, bony arms, with their red
elbows, over her chest. Her voice, as
grating and monotonous as a saw, drilled
into Josephine's head. "I will not have that

big, lazy girl taking food from the mouths of my children. I just will not have it. You have to find a way to get her on her way. She riles me, and I will not have her keep living here."

Josephine knew she could not go back. It would be a terrible blow to her pride, even if they would take her back. And then Lillian would make Pa pay for it. She would punish Pa in every way she knew how if he let his daughter return to the farm.

And finally, Pa would be even more eager than Lillian to see Josephine go.

Josephine had to face the sad fact that she had no real home to return to. No place where she was welcome or would probably ever be welcome again.

Josephine was almost too tired to eat supper that night. She had to force down the chicken, potatoes, and peas. She didn't want to hurt Aunt Lena's feelings by refusing to eat. But all she really wanted to do was go to bed.

Aunt Lena asked Josephine about her first day. Josephine was too tired to complain. Plus, she figured Aunt Lena wouldn't be very understanding. She had done the same work when she was Josephine's age. And she was determined that any young girl today could do the same. Josephine answered her question with a mere, "Fine."

Upstairs in the sleeping room, Prudence said, "Old Slattery was even worse than usual today because they just got a big order for men's shirts. When a big order comes in, he gets to be a regular slave driver, Jo." She was obviously trying to boost her new friend's spirits. "You picked a bad time to start work." She sat on the side of the bed brushing her long yellow hair.

Josephine was eager to go to sleep. But she was so tense and restless that she could not fall quickly into slumber. She looked at Prudence's pretty profile. She'll catch the eye of some flashy fellow who will take her away from all this drudgery, Josephine thought.

Josephine did not feel nearly so pretty. She thought her mother had been very beautiful. Ma often told Josephine she was pretty, but Josephine didn't believe it.

She thought it was only a mother's love speaking. Josephine knew some rich man would never come and sweep her away to his mansion. She wasn't even sure she wanted that to happen. Sometimes Josephine dreamed of being a nurse or a teacher. She wanted to help people. But that would require education. Sure, she could read and write and do simple arithmetic. But she didn't know how she would ever afford a college education.

Josephine crept out of bed and went to her carpetbag. She quietly dug out her doll. She thought holding the doll might help her fall asleep. Ma had given Josephine the doll when she was seven. And Josephine had felt like the luckiest girl in the world. She thought she could still feel her mom's love when she held the doll.

Prudence got into bed and fell asleep immediately. Josephine hugged her doll to her chest. In a few minutes she, too, had fallen asleep. The doll rose and fell with her breathing.

* * *

It came as a terrible shock when Prudence shook Josephine awake. "Time to get up, Jo!" Prudence said.

Josephine could see that it was still dark outside. Every bone in her body ached, and she didn't think she could get out of bed. But slowly she got up. She tucked her doll under the covers when she made the bed. Then she hurried to wash up and get dressed. When she went downstairs for breakfast, she felt like she was sleepwalking.

"Did you sleep well last night?" Aunt Lena asked.

"Yes," Josephine lied.

"You don't look it," Aunt Lena said. "You look like the wreck of the *Hesperus.*"

Ma had always described things as being as bad off as the wreck of the *Hesperus* too. Josephine was confused the first time she heard her mother say it. But she had informed Josephine that the *Hesperus* was a wrecked ship from a Longfellow poem. It was almost comforting to hear that expression again.

Aunt Lena smoothed back Josephine's

dark red hair and wrapped the bun tighter at the nape of her neck. Josephine used to love it when her mother braided her hair. No matter how carefully Josephine would braid her own hair, it never looked as nice as when Ma had done it. Now, though Aunt Lena was hardly like Ma, her attention brought tears to Josephine's eyes.

"Oh, Aunt L–l–ena," Josephine cried, "I miss Ma so much. I miss the farm and Addie and my friends. I . . . I . . . miss being home."

"Listen, child," Aunt Lena said, "you must say good-bye to your childhood. You're a young working woman now. You'll be all right. Do your best and be patient. And always be respectful to your bosses at the mill." Aunt Lena smiled then and looked a little more like her sister, Josephine's mother.

Suddenly, Josephine fled into Aunt Lena's arms and began to sob like a little girl. She couldn't go back to the mill and Mr. Slattery.

She couldn't spend another day in that foul-smelling, noisy, crowded, awful place.

3 "Now, stop this nonsense," Aunt Lena scolded. "Come on now. I have a nice basin of cold water. Wash your face, straighten your shoulders, and head off to work."

Josephine knew that Aunt Lena was only trying to help. But she was an obdurate woman. And what Josephine really wanted was some sympathy or comfort. She realized that she had no choice but to face that mill again. So she washed her face. She tried to remove the evidence of the tears. Then she ran to join Prudence and the dozens of other girls going to the mill.

When she arrived at the mill, Josephine first took a deep breath. Then she sat right down at her sewing machine and began working diligently. Surprisingly, it was much easier than yesterday. Yesterday everything had been new and frightening. Now Josephine attacked the stack of shirts with more experience, sewing the cut pieces together. But her pile of finished work still did not rise as quickly as Prudence's. Or even as quickly as Gladys Payton's who worked at her side.

Josephine looked from Gladys's pile to Gladys. Something was wrong with Gladys today. She looked even wearier and paler than the other girls.

"Ohhh," Gladys began to moan around mid-morning. She doubled over and clutched her stomach. "It hurts *so much!*" Bertha hurried over. "Shhh . . . hush, Gladys. Do you want Mr. Slattery hearing you and docking your pay?"

"Oh, Bertha," Gladys groaned, "I am so sick . . . ."

"No, you're not," Bertha said firmly. "We all have those stomach pains, and we just grit our teeth and go on working. Don't be a crybaby, Gladys. I'll bring you some water." Bertha hurried away and returned shortly with a cup of water. "Here, drink it down and keep working."

Gladys drank the water, but it seemed to do no good at all.

"I'm gonna faint," Gladys cried. As soon as she got the words out of her mouth, Gladys toppled over in her chair. She fell to the floor with a loud THUD.

Mr. Slattery came marching over. "What is this? This idiot has given me trouble before. She spends her nights drinking at parties, and then she reports to work too sick to do her job!"

Another girl said in a small voice, "Gladys doesn't drink. It's a female problem she suffers from, sir."

"Silence!" Mr. Slattery thundered. "Gladys is a lazy, drunken fool, and I want her out of here!"

Bertha lifted Gladys back onto her chair. Perspiration glistened on the girl's face. Her head rolled on her shoulders as if it were too heavy. She was as white as chalk.

"Are you all right, Gladys?" Bertha asked.

Gladys mumbled something that didn't make sense. Josephine watched with horror. The poor girl could be dying, for all they cared.

"Get her out of here, I said!" Mr. Slattery shouted. "Get somebody to help you carry her out, Bertha. I don't want her here another minute. Everyone is gawking!"

Josephine ran to Gladys's aid. She held Gladys on one side. Bertha held her on the other, and they dragged her outside. The cool, clean air hit her face. After a few minutes, Gladys seemed somewhat revived. "Oh, I'm better now," she said. "I can go back in and work. The pains in my stomach aren't as bad now." Fear of losing her job was more important to Gladys than her health now.

"Gladys, this is the third time something like this has happened," Bertha pointed out sternly. "Mr. Slattery is not willing to put up with it anymore. He doesn't want you back."

Gladys's eyes widened in terror. "Not today, or not *ever?*"

"Surely he'll change his mind when he gets over being angry," Josephine suggested. She felt pity for this poor girl she hardly knew.

Bertha shook her head. "Mr. Slattery never changes his mind. He's a very determined man."

"But what am I going to do?" Gladys sobbed.

"Go home to your family, Gladys," Bertha advised. "We have to get back to work. Mr. Slattery will fire all of us if we don't."

"I have no family," Gladys wailed. "I have to go back to the sewing machine. I'll work twice as fast and make up for the time I lost. I will. I swear I will."

"We have to go. I'm sorry," Bertha said.

Josephine followed Bertha back into the mill. She felt so sorry for Gladys, but what could she do?

"Back to work!" Mr. Slattery shouted as the two girls came in.

Gladys came back inside too. "Please, Mr. Slattery, give me another chance," she sobbed.

Horace Slattery's face flushed with anger. "I told you that you are finished here. Do you understand me? You're finished here! I told you the last time that if you continued your dissolute life and fell over the sewing machine like a common drunk, you were through," he said.

"Mr. Slattery, I swear I don't drink! I have never been drunk! Please, just let me work—" Gladys cried.

"Get out, or I will call the law to remove you," Mr. Slattery threatened. "I'll write a letter to every mill in town blacklisting you if you give me one more bit of trouble. That means no mill will hire you!" Gladys finally fled, sobbing uncontrollably. The room returned to the cacophony of the whirring machines and the cursing of Mr. Slattery as he goaded the workers on.

During the break for lunch, Josephine sat near Prudence and ate her sandwich. Josephine asked in a low tone, "What will happen to poor Gladys?"

Prudence shrugged her shoulders. "She's sickly. I don't think she's made for this type of work. Maybe she can get homework. You know, sewing by the task that you can do at home," she said.

"Does she really not have a family?" Josephine asked.

"Her father is a drunkard, and she ran away from him," Prudence said. "I don't think she knows where her family is now."

"Poor Gladys," Josephine said.

"What can we do? We're all in the same boat, Jo. We have to scramble to keep our heads above water. We're not the lucky ones. We're not young damsels spending our days reading poetry and taking dancing lessons," Prudence said coldly.

Josephine went back to work. Her pile of finished work grew. When Mr. Slattery came to inspect her work, he contented himself with just some muttering. Josephine herself saw great improvement in her work.

Josephine's mother had always told her that she was clever and could do anything she set her mind to. Josephine had always been too insecure to completely believe it. Now she surprised herself by mastering the sewing machine more quickly than she thought she would. The lessons she had learned from the sewing machine salesman on the farm were all coming back to her now.

But, as the day went by, the terrible ache returned to Josephine's shoulders. She didn't think she could sit like this another minute without screaming. But there were two hours left. Josephine longed to stop for just five minutes to stretch and relax.

But Josephine had to be careful. Mr. Slattery was ubiquitous. When a girl stopped working for a minute, Mr. Slattery would appear like a devil with a pitchfork. He seemed to have eyes in the back of his head. He always knew where idleness was lurking.

Josephine struggled through the last two hours. But she managed to survive until the end of the day. She waited while Mr. Slattery gave her work a final inspection.

"Not very good, but better," he snapped. He seemed to be sorry he couldn't heap more abuse on her head.

Josephine was relieved not to be the recipient of Mr. Slattery's wrath this time. She rushed into the fresh night air. She was eager to inhale air that wasn't clogged with cotton particles.

"Prudence, do you know where Gladys lives?" Josephine asked on the way home.

"Are you still thinking about her?" Prudence asked with a grimace. "She's 18 years old, Jo. She can find something. She isn't 15 like you."

"I'm 14," Josephine admitted.

Prudence turned and laughed. "Are you now? So you lied. Well, most of us do.

They don't like girls as young as 14. Some of those spinsters who go around making speeches about the plight of working children have made it difficult for the mill owners. They've heard stories of kids as young as five or six being chained to their machines for 16 hours. The mill owners are afraid one of us might be killed in a fire or an accident. And then the newspapers would catch on and cause more trouble for the mills. This one lady named Catherine Beecher has written all sorts of articles saying that women and children are being abused by the greedy rich. She thinks we should all be in school, not in factories. But things will never change," Prudence added coldly.

"They might change," Josephine said. She tried to remain hopeful. "I admire people who have pity for the less fortunate. I'd like to help other people if I ever get out of here."

"That's nice, Jo. You've got a good heart," Prudence said. "Right now I just want to help myself. I'm hungry. Let's hurry before the other girls get the biggest helpings," Prudence suggested.

"You go on ahead," Josephine told her. "I've got to do something real quick."

Prudence rushed off to wash up for supper.

Even though she was tired and hungry, Josephine searched out the boardinghouse where Gladys Payton lived. A cross landlady scornfully told Josephine that Gladys had already packed her things and left. "If she can't pay her way, then she can't stay here," the woman snapped. "I am not an almshouse."

Josephine reluctantly returned to her boardinghouse and joined Prudence and the other girls at supper. They had left her some hearty beef stew and green beans. She even had a little peach cobbler for dessert. But all the good food made Josephine worry about Gladys again. Josephine remained in the kitchen with Aunt Lena after the other girls had left. Josephine told Aunt Lena about Gladys and how sad she felt.

"Oh, Jo, don't fret over someone you don't even know. If they fired her, she was probably not a very hardworking girl anyway. I believe you get your just deserts in this world," Aunt Lena said.

Just then the vegetable vendor came to the back door. Aunt Lena bought a supply of potatoes, onions, green beans, beets, and carrots. The vendor began carrying the vegetables into the kitchen. Josephine continued on about Gladys. She remembered what Prudence had said about Boston. Trying to be optimistic, Josephine suggested that Gladys might get work in Boston. The vendor looked up with a wry grin at the mention of the city. "Are you going to Boston, young lady?" he asked Josephine.

"Oh, no, not me. But a friend might be," Josephine said.

"Ah," the vendor said, "Boston is a fine place for the rich, but God help you if you're poor. It's a bitter life indeed for them that has no money."

Aunt Lena frowned and said, "Is it any different anywhere in the world? No matter where we are, we must make our living by the sweat of our brows."

"But Boston is crowded with poor Irish immigrants. They'll do anything to make a few pennies. Little children sit and make flowers for five cents a day," the vendor said, unloading the last of his vegetables. He collected his money from Aunt Lena and left.

After he was gone, Josephine said, "I hope poor Gladys didn't go to Boston. It must be awful there."

Aunt Lena seemed ready to put an end to Josephine's words of concern. "I told you. Don't worry your head over some girl who is not even your kin, Josephine. Just be glad your own day at the factory went well. Bertha stopped by to tell me you are doing well. And I told her to send my thanks to Mr. Fergus, the man who owns the place. You can write a letter to your father on Sunday and tell him you are doing well. That will put his heart at ease," Aunt Lena said.

Josephine's mind drifted to Pa. With all the stress and concentration required at work, she had not really thought about anything else. She wondered what Pa would think if he knew about the mill. If he knew about Mr. Slattery or her aching back. If he knew about Gladys. "Do you think Pa worries about me, Aunt Lena?"

Josephine asked.

Aunt Lena looked clearly irritated. "Of course he does," she scolded. "Now head off to bed."

4 The rest of the week crawled by. The girls worked six days a week. And it seemed that Sunday would never come. When it did, Josephine could hardly believe it. What a luxury to lie in bed and then take her time washing and dressing! And how good it felt not having a 12-hour day of hard work ahead of her.

After breakfast, Josephine decided to write a letter to her father like Aunt Lena had suggested.

> Dear Father:
>
> I am working very hard. I have mastered the sewing machine, and my shirts now pass inspection. I believe I will keep this job. I know you would be proud if you could see what difficult work I do. The shirts I make look every bit as nice as those in the dry goods stores. I am not sick, but I am very tired. And I cough now more than I ever have. I think the bits of cotton get into our lungs.
>
> Your daughter, Josephine

Josephine and Prudence went into Baldwin at midday. They wanted to get as much fresh air into their lungs as possible. It felt so good to breathe in clean air not fouled by pungent smells and flying debris. The girls had brought a basket packed with chicken sandwiches and biscuits. They found a small grassy knoll by a small pond where ducks sailed around like little white ships. They sat down to eat and revel in the sunshine.

A young man was sitting on the opposite side of the pond. From time to time, he seemed to look at the girls.

"Look at that fellow over there," Prudence said. "He's quite ugly, but his clothes look nice. I wonder if he's rich."

Josephine giggled. The young man had a nose like a crow's beak and a long, skinny neck. "He is a flashy dresser. Maybe he's the son of a mill owner," Josephine said.

"How old do you think he is, Jo?" Prudence asked.

"Eighteen or nineteen," Josephine said.

"You think if I smile shyly in his direction, he'll notice me and introduce me to his rich family?" Prudence asked.

"Prudie! You said he was ugly!" Jo exclaimed.

"I don't care," Prudence said. "If he's rich and takes a liking to me, he can be ugly as a hedgehog. Think of it, Jo. If we began courting now, I could be married by the time I'm 18."

"I may not marry at all," Josephine said.

Prudence turned and stared at Josephine. "What on earth are you saying? You want to be a spinster? Who's going to take care of you? If you're a rich spinster, it's well and good to be alone. You could travel anywhere and find things to do for fun. But when you're poor like us, you have to find a husband!"

"I want to save my money. I'd like to go to school and learn to be a teacher," Josephine said. "I have aspirations. I don't want a humdrum life."

"A teacher!" Prudence gasped.

"Or maybe a writer like Catherine Beecher. I want to help people. I want to feel like I make a difference in the world. Instead of just putting new shirts on people who don't need them. Maybe someday people might say, 'Listen to that Josephine Thorpe. She has important things to say,' " Josephine said.

"Shhh," Prudence commanded, "he's looking over here. He's looking at me. Do you see how he's stealing glances?" Prudence reached up and gave her pale cheeks quick pinches to restore their color. "How do I look? Should I smile at him, or would that be bold?"

Josephine giggled again. "I don't think he's looking at us at all. I think he's watching the ducks."

Prudence sighed. "Well, he's probably not rich anyway. Look at his silly coat. It doesn't fit him. If he were truly rich, he would have a coat made by a tailor. His coat hangs on him like a coat on a scarecrow," she said.

The girls finished their sandwiches and began to walk slowly along the pond. "Why can't we spend every day like this?" Prudence remarked. "Strolling and talking. It doesn't seem fair that we have to toil like slaves, and other girls spend all day practicing music or reading French."

Two young men came toward them

from the opposite direction. They were rougher looking than the boy they had seen earlier. And their lips were blackened by tobacco.

"Ah, look at the fair doves," one of the youths laughed.

Prudence grabbed Josephine's hand and whispered fiercely, "Walk very quickly and don't even look at them."

When they passed the young men, Prudence said, "They work at the print works. They're very coarse, and they spend all their wages on tobacco and liquor. To be a wife to a man like that would be a fate worse than death."

Josephine nodded, but she didn't quite understand. Her father was a good, hardworking man. But he drank sometimes and used tobacco. He was also uneducated. Many might consider him coarse because he didn't know much about manners. But he was a good husband to Josephine's mother, and now to Lillian. Josephine's father had never been unkind to man or beast, not that Josephine knew of anyway.

"My father is like those two," Prudence said bitterly. "Gladys's father too. My ma's life is miserable."

"What's your pa like?" Josephine asked. "Is he mean?"

"My pa is a cruel man. He's awful, Jo," Prudence said. A shudder ran through her body as she said again, "Awful."

Josephine shook her head sadly as she thought about how unfair the world could be.

For the rest of the day, Josephine read a book, and Prudence lay staring at the clouds. Finally, regrettably, they had to return to the boardinghouse. After supper, Josephine went to bed, dreading the next day. The next relief, the next Sunday, seemed so far away.

Too soon morning came, and Josephine was scrambling to be at work on time. She knew if she was late, her meager pay would be docked. If Mr. Slattery was in a bad mood, she could even be fired.

As the girls took their places at the machines, Mr. Slattery appeared in the center of the room. He demanded quiet so he could make an important announcement.

"Production has been down here at the

factory, and the owners are very disappointed," he said. "You girls have all been sluggards."

Prudence spat, "Liar!" just under her breath.

"Because of that, because of your own laziness, profits are down. So your wages must be cut by 15 percent," Mr. Slattery said.

A gasp spread through the ranks of the girls like a balloon that had lost its air. Fifteen percent less would mean that most girls would lose 45 to 50 cents a week. They were already finding it hard to pay the $1.50 a week at the boardinghouses. Very little was left for clothing, savings, or a little recreation on Sundays.

The girls began to grumble to one another.

"Stop that muttering and go back to work," Mr. Slattery shouted. He waited for the talking to subside. "You brought this misfortune on yourselves. You are lucky you're not all fired. Plenty of girls are eager to work for far less than you are making."

Josephine was stunned by the injustice of it all. Indignation swept over her like a quick shudder in the cold. How could they cut wages that were already so low? Everyone had been working hard. Everyone could see that more shirts, trousers, and dresses were going out to the railroad cars than ever before. They were being sent to stores all over the country. The owners of the factory just wanted more profits. They were greedy. They were sure that they could squeeze more money from the poor, overworked girls.

Conversation was forbidden in the sewing room. So only after the final bell, as the girls streamed out into the darkness, could they talk about the pay cut.

"It's so rotten unfair," Prudence cried. "How can that happen?"

"You must understand," Bertha said, "these are not good times. When the Civil War was going on, this mill did a splendid business. They made clothing for the soldiers. Mr. Slattery told me it was the best of times. But now clothing isn't selling like it was."

Prudence glared at Bertha but said no more. Josephine knew that nearly everybody in the mill suspected that Bertha's loyalties were totally with the mill owners and Mr. Slattery. The girls did not trust her. They feared that whatever they said to her might be whispered in Mr. Slattery's ear tomorrow. And the girl who expressed herself would be fired.

Bertha left the group, and Prudence and Josephine walked on alone toward the boardinghouse. Prudence said, "She's a snitch, Bertha is. I hate her. She'd cut our throats if it meant another dollar for her."

Josephine wasn't sure. Bertha was always kind to her. She was very helpful when Josephine was struggling to learn the machine. Josephine thought that she couldn't really blame Bertha. She was a victim of the system too. If she took the side of the sewing machine girls, she would be fired.

When Josephine and Prudence got to the boardinghouse, they quickly washed up and went to supper. Everyone at the table was eager to talk about the pay cut. Aunt Lena set out scrambled eggs and ham along with hot buttered biscuits. But the girls could barely eat. Their mouths were busy cursing the owners of the mill.

"They'll slowly cut down our wages until we're nothing but slaves," Prudence said.

"We're already slaves," a girl named Roxanne said. "When I don't work quickly enough, Slattery hits me. If I complained to the police, would they listen? No, they're on the side of the owners."

"We're like machines without souls. And we're earning starvation wages. Now there will be even less," another girl, Leticia, said.

A dark-haired girl named Rosie nodded and said, "What are we going to do about it? Who has an idea about what we can do?"

"What can we do?" Josephine asked. "If we protest, we'll be fired. And then they can blacklist us."

Prudence turned sharply to Josephine. "So we just do nothing and suffer the injustices? We're just s'posed to slave away for less and less money until we die of overwork?" she demanded.

Josephine shrugged. She didn't have the answer. All her life, she had seen unfairness. When Josephine's father had used the railroad to ship his produce, the rates were often raised for no reason. It would eat up all his profits. And he could do nothing because there was just one railroad. If he didn't use it, then his produce would rot in the fields.

Most unfair was what happened to Josephine's mother. When her mother got sick, the family had no money for a doctor. By the time she was desperately ill, they finally convinced a doctor to come. They had to promise him part of their crop. But it was too late to save her.

Josephine didn't know what to do about injustice, even though it made her angry.

"Well," a girl named Nanette said, "all I know is that even less money is better than no wages at all. And when times are better, maybe we'll get raises. I'll miss that 50 cents as much as anybody else. But I know I can't live without any wages at all."

"She's right," a girl named Blanche said. "We have to just take it. We're like dumb, driven cattle. We have no choice."

Aunt Lena put out more ham and eggs and said, "Listen to Nanette. She is very young, but she's wise. Don't let these firebrands lead you astray. Many years ago there was a labor uprising over in Lowell. And all the troublemakers got for rabble-rousing was losing their jobs and being blacklisted all over Massachusetts."

After supper Josephine and Prudence went up to their room. Prudence took down her blond hair and brushed it slowly.

"I wish there was a way we could strike back, Prudie. But they've got all the power. I feel weak and hopeless," Josephine said.

"You are only a child, Jo. You don't know yet how to stand up for yourself, and that's to be expected. When I was 14, I didn't know much either," Prudence said.

"But what about now? Do you have an idea?" Josephine asked.

A terrible smile danced on Prudence's lips. "We're like flies, and they're like a large, powerful beast. The flies can't defeat the beast, but the flies can sting. Oh, yes. They'll be sorry for that 50 cents they're taking out of our hides!"

5   Josephine was awakened near midnight by Prudence climbing out of bed.

"Prudie?" Josephine whispered. "Is there something wrong?"

"Stomachache," Prudence said. "It's nothin'. Go back to sleep."

Josephine turned over and tried to go back to sleep, but she couldn't. She lay awake for almost an hour, wondering why Prudence hadn't returned. Then she thought of that terrible smile on Prudence's face last night when she had talked about making the mill sorry.

Finally Prudence came tiptoeing back into the room. She got undressed and slipped into bed. Josephine was too afraid to ask Prudence what she had been doing. She wasn't sure she wanted to know.

When the girls reached the mill the next morning, there was high excitement in the air. Mr. Slattery was running around the room with one of the owners, a sliver of an old man named Mr. Fergus. Nobody said anything to the girls in the morning, but someone overheard Bertha talking to Mr. Slattery. After that the story spread like wildfire.

A packing case full of women's dresses waiting to be shipped to Chicago had been torched last night. Someone had poured kerosene on the contents and set fire to it. The firemen got there quickly, and only half a dozen dresses were burned. But all the rest were scorched or damaged in some way. At the very least, they smelled terrible and would have to be thrown out.

By noon, Mr. Slattery and Mr. Fergus had ordered the bell tolled to get everyone's attention.

Mr. Fergus made the announcement. "A shocking incident of vandalism took place here last night," he said in a dry, crackling voice that itself sounded like flames eating through brush. "Dresses, ready to ship, were deliberately destroyed. If anyone here knows anything about this act of sabotage, now is the time to speak up."

A few girls gasped in shock, but most looked indifferent. Josephine forced herself to stare at her sewing machine. She didn't want to exchange a look with Prudence for fear she'd be observed.

Josephine remembered Prudence's hour-long midnight disappearance, and she feared it had something to do with the vandalism. The thought of it sent chills up Josephine's spine.

"If anyone here is responsible for the vandalism," Mr. Slattery said, "you will be caught. Do not think for a moment that you will get away with this criminal action. You will be caught, and you will be sent to prison for a long, long time."

Josephine was terrified for Prudence. What if she had done it? Josephine had heard of harsh sentences being handed out for offenses far less serious than setting fire to a crate of clothing.

"If the vile culprit sits at a sewing machine right now pretending to be innocent," Mr. Slattery hissed, "consider that your freedom will be shortlived. As surely as the sun rises and sets, you will be caught!"

"Return to your work now," Mr. Fergus said in a monotone, "and ponder what Mr. Slattery has said."

Josephine labored diligently at her pile of work. She did not dare even glance at

Prudence. She was afraid something might be read into the glance. She didn't want to implicate Prudence or herself.

At lunch, Prudence didn't seem the least bit scared or even nervous. She didn't even bring up the subject of the fire. "There's a concert tomorrow night. I think I'll go," she said. "The nicest men are in those crowds. And the richest." Josephine just looked at Prudence quizzically.

Even as the two girls walked home after work, Prudence was very blithe. She did not mention the fire at all. Neither did Josephine. After supper the girls were alone in their room. Suddenly Prudence looked at Josephine and said, "You think I set the fire, don't you?"

"I never said that," Josephine said. Even though she feared she was wrong, she turned to Prudence and said, "Oh, Prudie, you couldn't have done such a thing!"

"I did so," Prudence said. She laughed and spun around the center of the room like a ballerina, her blond hair flying.

"Prudie, no!" Josephine cried. "How could you?"

"I was very careful. I made sure the box

of dresses was far from anything else so there wouldn't be a bad fire. I'm only telling you this because I trust you, Jo," Prudence said. "Don't you see why I had to do it? We have no other way of striking back at them. If we protest the cut in our wages, they'll fire us. If we walk off the job, they'll blacklist us."

"But still, Prudie, it was a bad thing to do," Josephine said.

Prudence could tell that Josephine was troubled. "I had to do it. Nobody saw me. They'll never pin it on me. And those greedy men have paid for taking another wage cut out of our hides," Prudence said proudly.

"But wasn't there another way?" Josephine asked.

"Like what?" Prudence answered. She sat down beside Josephine on the bed. "Listen to me, Jo. Nobody gets away with doing rotten things if I can help it. Like my father. He would get crazy with rum and he'd beat us all, especially our ma. He'd beat her bloody. Her face would look like a side of fresh meat. One night he came home fighting drunk. I ran and hid in the barn. But Ma screamed like I'd never heard her scream. And so I got a big piece of timber, I went in the house, and I hit him with it. I hit him in the legs, and I busted his right leg. He still limps.

"The doctor came and cussed him out for being so drunk that he fell and busted his leg. To this day he doesn't know for sure that it was me. He always looked at me a little funny after that, though. I think he was too humiliated to ask. But I'm glad I did it. He stopped hitting Ma that night. And he limps now. So when he comes after Ma and the kids, it's easier for them to get away . . . ." Prudence laughed then, clasping her knees and rocking back and forth on the bed.

Josephine didn't know what to say, so she just looked at Prudence with a kind of wonder.

"You think I'm awful, don't you, Jo?" Prudence asked.

"I don't know what to think, Prudie. I just know you shouldn't have started the fire," Josephine said, taking down her long red hair. She crawled into bed. She was scared for Prudence more than anything else. It wasn't only that Prudence was her friend, but she was her only real friend. If something happened to her, Josephine knew she would be even more alone.

And that scared her.

During lunch the next day at the mill, Bertha came and tapped Josephine on the shoulder. "Josephine, come into the office with me, please." Josephine froze with fear.

Did they know something about the fire? Josephine wondered.

Josephine sat down on an uncomfortable wooden chair in the office. Bertha sat behind a big, heavy oak desk. Bertha looked very important sitting there. She look at Josephine with condescension in her eyes. Obviously she was much more important than Josephine had thought.

"Yesterday when the pay cut was announced, there was some grumbling among the girls," Bertha said. "I have a list of the names of rebellious girls."

Josephine was sickened. Prudence was right. How could Bertha be a spy against the other girls?

"Well," Bertha said smiling, "you'll be glad to know you are not on this list." It felt like a kiss from a hated cousin with foul breath to be in Bertha's good graces.

"But talking is forbidden in the sewing room," Josephine said. "How could anyone have heard rebellious talk?"

Bertha's smile widened, making her look evil. "Ah, but some of our girls are very loyal to the mill. They tell us about rebellion spoken in the boardinghouses. And a word to the wise, Josephine. Such loyalty is always rewarded."

Josephine's mind was spinning. There were eight girls at the boardinghouse. Since Josephine and Prudence were obviously not the snitches, one of the other six had to be. How dreadful, Josephine thought. Which girl was it? It had to be either Violet, Blanche, Nanette, Rosie, Catherine, or Leticia. She didn't want to even think about it.

Bertha leaned forward. "Josephine, if you could give me some useful information on Prudence Kinney, one of the girls heard making hateful comments, then you would be handsomely rewarded. You see, we must catch the culprit who started the fire. And we feel it was most likely done by a vindictive sewing machine operator. Your reward would equal a month's pay, dear, and nobody need be the wiser . . . ." Bertha said.

Josephine felt as if she could vomit at the very thought of betraying a fellow worker. She knew lying was wrong, but she couldn't turn Prudence in. Josephine just couldn't do that to her. Or to any of the other girls who were suffering under the unfair treatment of the mill owners. "I can't help you, Bertha. I don't have any information," Josephine said.

"Josephine," Bertha said. Her whole demeanor changed from kindly to stern. "If it should later be discovered that you withheld information, you will, of course, lose your job. And you will be blacklisted."

Josephine stared at Bertha with something close to hatred. She was wicked, Josephine thought. "I'm sorry, Bertha, but I don't know anything. May I go back to work now? I have a lot of work to do."

"Yes, go," Bertha said.

Josephine returned to her sewing machine, carefully avoiding even a glance in Prudence's direction. But later, as the girls walked home together in the darkness, Josephine said, "Bertha questioned me about the fire. She knows what was said at supper in the boardinghouse. She knows you made disloyal statements about the pay cut. Bertha knows what every one of us said at supper last night."

Prudence's eyes narrowed with rage. "Oh, that detestable snake! Did you get any idea who the snitch might be, Josephine?"

"No. But we must be careful what we say at the supper table," Josephine said. "She offered me money to give her information about who started the fire."

Prudence threw an arm around Josephine's shoulders. "I love you better than my own sisters, Jo. I can trust you. You are a true-blue friend. When I marry some rich man and go live in a mansion, I'll take you there with me. I promise," she said.

Josephine did not smile. "Just promise me, Prudie, that you will do nothing else to get us in trouble. I can't bear something happening to you."

Prudence grinned. "I promise you I will not set any more fires," she said. "But if I find the snitch who's betraying us to Bertha, I may beat her senseless!"

6 Josephine was more tired than usual the next day. She had a cold, and she was fighting a fever as she sat at the sewing machine. Nothing was worse than being sick at work. Never had 12 hours seemed so long! Once or twice Josephine feared she would faint from exhaustion, but she remembered how quickly Gladys was fired for being ill. So Josephine snatched a minute when nobody was looking to hang her head down and bring more blood to her brain. Her grandmother had told her once that it could ward off a fainting spell.

Josephine didn't want to be suspicious of her fellow workers, but she found herself speculating on who the snitch might be. Thinking about Bertha's accomplice helped take her mind off her aching body. If Bertha lingered at Rosie's table, Josephine thought Rosie was the snitch. If Bertha seemed friendly to Nanette, Josephine wondered if she was the snitch.

When the day finally ended, Josephine managed to drag herself down the street toward the boardinghouse.

"I'm going to a concert tonight," Prudence said. "I can't afford it, but I'm going anyway. This just might be the night I meet someone rich."

"I'm just going home and getting some chicken soup before I go to bed," Josephine said.

"Everyone is sick in the mill," Prudence said. "It's the horrid air."

Josephine quickly drank the chicken soup Aunt Lena had made for her. What Prudence had said was true. Many of the girls were sniffling and hacking. It was bitter cold in the room, and the air was always foul. It was no wonder they were dropping like flies.

After Josephine went to bed, Aunt Lena came in to check on her. She felt Josephine's brow and said, "You aren't very warm. I'm sure you'll be all well in the morning, Josephine."

Josephine lay back on her pillow and sighed. She remembered when she was sick as a little girl. Her mother would always fuss over her. Josephine had felt so loved, so safe. She remembered how her mother was always washing or cleaning, and her hands smelled of lye soap. Or sometimes Ma's hands smelled of apples when she was making applesauce, or some other good smell. Just feeling her mother's hands on her brow had made Josephine feel better, no matter how ill she was. "Aunt Lena," Josephine said, "I miss my ma."

"Well," Aunt Lena said, "she died a long time ago. You should be over that by now. Land sakes, it's been—what?—four years? I lost my mother at about that age. And by the time I was your age, I scarcely remembered her."

"I remember my ma, and I miss her terribly," Josephine said. She was angry that Aunt Lena had told Josephine to forget her mother. She didn't want to forget her—ever!

"Just put those things out of your mind, Josephine, and plan for the future. You can save your money and one day meet a nice gentleman. Then you can have a family of your own," Aunt Lena said.

"I loved it when Ma would braid my hair. Ma braided my hair in such a lovely way," Josephine said, lost in her memories. "The braids were so nice and even. Ma and I would talk while she did it. I felt so close to her."

"You are 14 years old, Josephine. It's time to put away childish memories," Aunt Lena said sternly. "You want to be a mature girl, don't you?"

Josephine decided to change the subject. It did no good to argue with Aunt Lena. She was determined to make Josephine put her childhood behind her. And Josephine was equally determined never to forget her past.

"Aunt Lena, do you know what I found out at the mill today? There are girls who work there and listen at supper to what the girls say in the boardinghouses. And then they tell Bertha at the mill. They spy on us and make trouble with the bosses. Can you imagine anyone being so evil?" Josephine asked.

"Josephine," Aunt Lena scolded, "such things are none of your business. Just mind that you never say anything anywhere that you wouldn't be willing to shout from the housetops. Do not take part in complaining and gossiping."

"But the mill is cutting our pay by 45 cents a week, Aunt Lena. And we must work just as hard. Don't you think that's unfair?" Josephine asked.

"Business is not good at the mills," Aunt Lena said. "The owners have no choice but to cut the wages. When I read the newspapers, I see all sorts of dire stories of business failures. Thousands of firms are in trouble. Have some pity for those poor men who have invested in factories, who provide jobs. These are the venerable men who are paying your way." Aunt Lena continued her lecture. "In my day, we were thankful for the work at the cotton mill, though it was hard and dreadful," she said.

Josephine sighed. "I suppose so," she said. When Aunt Lena was gone, Josephine hugged her doll to her chest and went to sleep. It was all that comforted her now.

Prudence returned home just after 10:00, annoying Aunt Lena who wanted all the boarders in by ten. Josephine heard Aunt Lena upbraiding Prudence.

"We cannot have girls straggling in at all

hours. This house has a good reputation, and I will not have girls coming in late with liquor on their breath. Mind me, Prudence. Any more of this, and you shall be bounced out of here in a hurry."

"Oh, ma'am," Prudence said in a contrite voice, "I have an awful head cold, and someone suggested I take a sip of whiskey for the fever. I have never tasted liquor before, and I never will again. Even for medicinal purposes!"

"Well, see that you don't," Aunt Lena said sharply. "This is a boardinghouse for decent, upright young women. Not immoral drunkards."

Prudence went up to the sleeping room. After she closed the door, she laughed heartily. "I fooled the old thing. She thinks I took the whisky for my health!"

"Prudie, are you just getting back from the concert?" Josephine asked.

"Oh, I didn't even get to the concert. I met this wonderful fellow—Orville Lansing. And he gave me a ride in his wagon. He said that he's very rich, but he doesn't want anyone to know. So he rides around in this smelly wagon. We went to a tavern, and he bought me a fine meal—we had oysters, Jo! And then he bought me a drink. Oh, I felt like I was riding on a magic carpet! Orville said he likes me and wants to see me again," Prudence said.

"Are you sure he's rich?" Josephine asked.

"Oh, yes, as rich as Midas. He's just visiting here in Baldwin. He lives in Boston, and he has a handsome house there."

There was a knock on the door of the sleeping room. When Prudence opened the door, Nanette was there in her nightgown. "Will you be quiet in here?" she asked crossly. "You are keeping the rest of us awake. Just because you are drunk, Prudence, you have no right to disturb us!"

"I am not drunk," Prudence snapped. "You are a horrid little witch to say that I am."

"Prudie, shhhh," Josephine pleaded.

"Nobody shushes me," Prudence said, her face hot with anger.

When Nanette was gone, Prudence said, "I'd not be surprised if she was the one spying on us for the mill. She's just the kind who would do it. I'd like to dump the chamber pot on her head!"

"Prudie, we don't have any proof. Let's just forget it," Josephine pleaded. "I don't want any more trouble."

"She'd better not go behind our backs to the bosses," Prudence said darkly. "We're down-and-outers, Jo. We've got to stand up for ourselves."

"Prudie, if you're caught doing something wrong, you'll be sent to some awful prison!" Josephine groaned.

"Nobody will ever catch me," Prudence boasted.

Prudence crawled into bed. Josephine was tired but found it hard to fall asleep. Prudence was making her very nervous.

Josephine slept fitfully all night, but in the morning she felt a little better. The chicken soup must have helped, she thought.

After arriving at work, Josephine and Prudence were told that Nanette Strong was promoted. She would work as Bertha's assistant. Prudence glared over at Josephine as if this was proof positive that her suspicions were right. But that wasn't the worst of it. Nanette used her new position to make life miserable for Prudence.

"These collars are not acceptable," she said, snatching up Prudence's work. "Rip them out and do them right."

"There isn't time," Prudence said. "If I rip them, I won't finish before the bell."

Nanette sneered. "Then you'll work past quitting time and at no additional wages. You can't expect the mill to suffer for your mistakes."

"Let me resew some of the shirts," Josephine said.

"You have your own work," Nanette said sharply. She quickly came over to examine Josephine's work. "Ah, I see why you two are thick as thieves. You both do sloppy work. The side seams on these dresses are terrible. Rip them out and do them right!"

The bell rang, and the rest of the girls hurried out. But Josephine and Prudence had to stay at their machines to finish the work Nanette had not passed. They worked for an extra hour before they finally finished.

There was no one in the mill now but Mr. Slattery, Bertha, Nanette, and Josephine and Prudence. Josephine started to leave. She was so exhausted that she wondered how she would make it home.

She never saw exactly how the trouble started. But when she looked to see if Prudence was coming along, she saw Prudence and Nanette in a wild hair-pulling match. Prudence was getting the best of it until Bertha joined in, and then it was two against one. Bertha's hammy fists were pounding Prudence when Josephine rushed over. She caught hold of Bertha's hair and pulled hard so she would stop hitting Prudence.

Suddenly, Horace Slattery appeared. His face was dark with rage. "Stop it!" he screamed.

Prudence gave Nanette a violent shove, and the other girl skidded across the floor.

"You, you," Mr. Slattery gasped, "you shall be arrested and thrown into prison!" He was pointing at Prudence.

"She attacked me first," Prudence cried. "Nanette insulted and taunted me. I was only defending myself!"

Bertha glanced at Josephine, who had yanked her hair so hard that she now had a headache. "That one must go," Bertha said. She pointed at Josephine.

"You are both fired," Mr. Slattery snapped. "Prudence Kinney and Josephine Thorpe, you are never to return to this mill. What's more, I shall write a letter describing your criminal behavior. All other mill owners will be warned against you. You are very fortunate that the law has not been called. You two would be tossed into prison where you belong."

Josephine was sick. She couldn't believe what she had heard. She had lost her job. And the blacklisting would prevent her from finding another job in Baldwin. Josephine would not get wages anymore. What was she going to do? Aunt Lena wanted $1.50 a week for room and board. Where would it come from now?

Josephine began to cry, "Mr. Slattery, please. I need this job. I didn't mean to hurt Bertha. It was just that Nanette and Bertha both were pounding on Prudence. And I just wanted it to stop!"

7 "Begone with you," Slattery thundered. "If you two are not out of here in two minutes, I shall summon the law!"

"But I need this job," Josephine cried. Prudence grabbed her hand and pulled her along, out of the mill and into the dark street. The realization of what had just happened released a deluge of tears down Josephine's face. "Ohh, what will happen to us?" she moaned.

"Don't worry," Prudence said. "We'll come out all right. It's just a lucky thing that Orville Lansing is my friend now. He's very rich, and he said he came to Baldwin on business. His father probably owns a mill. We can get jobs there."

"Do you know where he's staying? Oh, Prudie, I've only saved two dollars. How far will two dollars go?" Josephine said.

"Orville said he's staying at the Baldwin Inn. They have nice rooms there. We'll go there right now and find him. I know he'll help us. He has a good heart," Prudence said.

The Baldwin Inn was a three-story brick building with nice furniture in the lobby. Prudence led the way inside and strode up to the desk. "We're looking for a guest who's staying here. Mr. Orville Lansing," Prudence said. She turned and gave Josephine an encouraging smile.

The desk clerk searched his registry and shook his head. "Nobody here by that name."

"Are you sure?" Prudence asked. "He said he was staying here."

Prudence turned and smiled again. But this smile wasn't quite as confident.

The clerk took another quick glance through his book. "I'm sorry, but he's not here," he said.

Prudence and Josephine went back out on the street. "Oh dear, I hope he hasn't gone back to Boston already," Prudence said. "But he liked me so very much, I'm sure he would have told me. It must be some kind of mix-up. Come on, Jo, we'll find him." Prudence grabbed Josephine's arm and began to drag her along.

Josephine stopped in the middle of the street. The desperation of the whole situation was beginning to set in. "Oh, Prudie, what am I going to tell Aunt Lena?

She's going to be so angry with me. Last night she gave me a lecture on how we need to be grateful to our bosses for giving us jobs. And now we were caught fighting. We've been fired and disgraced!" Josephine said.

"Oh, hush, Jo. We had to defend ourselves. Nanette was harassing me somethin' awful as I walked out. And I couldn't help grabbing her ugly hair and giving it a yank. And then she came at me like a demon. And Bertha was about to kill me. If you hadn't pitched in, I think they would've pounded me to death," Prudence said. She once again grabbed Josephine's arm and pulled her along.

They stopped at many places asking about Orville Lansing, but nobody knew of him. Finally, they came to a tavern at the edge of town. Prudence and Josephine went inside the dark establishment. Prudence asked an old man behind the bar, "Excuse me, but do you happen to know Orville Lansing?"

"You don't mean Orville Pruitt, do you?" the man asked.

"What does Orville Pruitt look like?"

Prudence asked. She was starting to get excited. "I s'pose I could've gotten the name mixed-up. The Orville I know has thick dark hair and fine blue eyes. And he is very, very handsome," Prudence said.

"Mmm, I suppose it could be him," the old man said.

"Where can we find him?" Prudence asked. Her eyes were shining. She couldn't wait to find the man that would solve all of their problems.

"He drives a big wagon," the old man said. "You can smell the wagon a mile off. Just go down the alley and most likely you'll see it parked behind the boardinghouses. Oftentimes he's sleepin' in the wagon at night . . . ."

Josephine exchanged a look with Prudence. "Why would a rich young man drive a smelly wagon and sleep in it?" she asked.

"Oh, never mind. Orville doesn't want people to know who he really is. I told you that," Prudence said. "Come on, Jo. Wait 'til you meet him. You'll like him as much as I did."

They walked down the dim alley until

they saw the wagon parked behind an old boardinghouse. Most of the boardinghouses in Baldwin were whitewashed regularly, but this one had not seen paint in a long time. The men who lived here were down-and-outers. One of them had a patch over his eye, and another had just one arm. They were Civil War veterans. Ever since the war had ended eight years ago, luckless men whose bodies had been disfigured in the war roamed the countryside. They would pick up whatever work they could find. They were called "Weary Willies" and "Tired Tims." Some were not physically disabled. The scars were in their minds. Josephine wondered now if Orville was one of them.

As they approached the wagon, they could see that someone was sleeping in there under a pile of blankets.

"Orville?" Prudence called out hesitantly.

A head emerged from the blankets. "Yeah . . . wha . . .?" he said. A faint smile came to his lips when he saw the pretty girl. "Um . . . Prudie, right?"

Josephine looked at Prudence. "I think he's had a little too much to drink."

"Orville, what are you doing sleeping in the wagon? Why aren't you down at the inn?" Prudence asked.

"Uh . . . well, Prudie, I mighta lied a lil' bit," Orville said. "I, uh . . . pick up refuse for the shops and the houses. But it's good, honest work and . . ."

Prudence glared at Orville and cried, "You said you were rich and lived in Boston!"

Orville Pruitt looked sad and humbled. But then he brightened at the memory of something meritorious he had once done. "Prudie," he said, "I fought at Shiloh."

Prudence turned and raced through the darkness with Josephine running after her. "The nerve of him to lie about his wealth," she fumed. "Oh, that wicked liar! The world is filled with wicked people, Jo," she yelled as she kept running down the street.

Josephine grabbed Prudence's arm. "Stop, Prudie. We have to go back to the boardinghouse. Aunt Lena has some influence in town. That's how I got the job at the mill. We must tell Aunt Lena exactly what happened, and maybe she can smooth things over," Josephine said. "Maybe if Aunt Lena pleaded for us with the owner of the mill, we might get another chance."

"No," Prudence almost screamed. "I won't grovel before those horrible people. How can you even think such a thing?"

"Prudie, we need wages to live," Josephine cried. "If we've lost our jobs and are blacklisted, we'll starve and have to live on the streets!" Josephine finally convinced Prudence that they had no choice. They had to face Aunt Lena.

When the girls reached the boardinghouse, it had been almost two hours since they were fired from the mill. Aunt Lena waited for them as they came into the front room. She got up from her chair, her arms folded. Anger flashed in her eyes. "Bertha has been here. She told me of your shocking misbehavior," she said. "Josephine, sit down. As for you, Prudence," her gaze struck Prudence like a blow, "get your things together by morning. You shall be out of here early tomorrow morning. You may spend the night here because I wouldn't even turn out a dog. But I do not want to see your face by the time the sun comes up."

Josephine gasped. "Aunt Lena, please!"

"Silence!" Aunt Lena snapped without even looking at Josephine.

"Fine!" Prudence shot back. "I hate this dirty old place anyway. The halls smell and the bedding isn't clean. The food isn't fit to eat. And there are bugs in the sleeping rooms." Prudence turned to Josephine, "Jo, when I leave in the morning, you're welcome to come along. We'll surely find a better place than this."

"No such thing, you depraved girl," Aunt Lena shouted. "This child will not go with you. You have led my niece astray. But I shall undo the damage you did, you corrupt and vile creature!"

Aunt Lena turned her back on Prudence to face Josephine. Then Prudence stormed from the room and marched angrily up the stairs.

Josephine was trembling so hard she almost bit her lip. "Please, Aunt Lena. What happened at the mill wasn't Prudie's fault. You see—" Josephine began to explain when the hairbrush in Aunt Lena's hand hit with full force against Josephine's face.

"Don't you speak that vile girl's name again! Don't try to justify her wild and brutal behavior. Or your own antics in defending her. Bertha told me how Prudence was angry at being reprimanded for shoddy work. And she began tearing at Nanette's hair like a wildcat. She told me how Prudence was being disciplined in a proper way for her outburst when you attacked Bertha in the same disorderly fashion," Aunt Lena said.

"Aunt Lena, Bertha is lying," Josephine said. She couldn't believe Bertha would twist the truth so much! Or that her aunt would believe Bertha over her own niece!

Aunt Lena caught hold of Josephine's hair, giving her head a violent shake. "Silence! I will hear no more of this. Bertha told me how Prudence has been poisoning the girls against the mill. Bertha is almost sure it was Prudence who started that fire. The girls at the mill are treated with kindness and charity. And this is how the generous owners are repaid!"

"No, you see—" Josephine started again. Once more the hard bristles of the hairbrush struck her in the face. Josephine's face was bruised and hot. And the pain stung her to her bones.

"Aunt Lena," Josephine sobbed.

Aunt Lena seized Josephine's thin arm and dragged her into the kitchen. The strong older woman took two wooden chairs and shoved them together.

"Kneel down and lie across the chairs, Josephine," Aunt Lena commanded.

Josephine was so frightened that she did as she was told. At once, blows from the hairbrush rained down on her shoulders, her back, and her head.

"Are you sorry for your disgraceful behavior, child?" Aunt Lena demanded when she paused in the beating.

"I didn't do anything," Josephine sobbed.

The beating continued. Except now the hairbrush was replaced by a leather strap. "Are you sorry?" Aunt Lena repeated.

"Y-yes, I'm sorry," Josephine cried.

"Are you sorry for your disgraceful and ungrateful behavior at the mill toward your bosses?" Aunt Lena demanded. She was unremitting in her beatings.

"Yes," Josephine sobbed.

"Are you sorry for following the bad example of that she-devil, Prudence Kinney?" Aunt Lena asked.

"Y-yes," Josephine cried.

"And from this moment forward, you will do what I tell you to make amends for your transgressions?" Aunt Lena asked sharply.

"Y-yes," Josephine promised, tears flooding down her cheeks. She could barely get the one-word reply out.

"You will sleep here on the kitchen floor tonight. I will not have you spending another minute with that evil girl," Aunt Lena said. She dropped a thin blanket and a mat on the floor.

Josephine washed her face in a basin of cold water as Aunt Lena set a dish of cold potatoes on the table. "This was left over from supper," Aunt Lena said.

Josephine had no appetite. She had never felt so miserable in all her life. "I must go home," she finally said. "I'll write a letter to my father and tell him I'll be coming home."

"You are not welcome there," Aunt Lena told her.

"I know my father would take me back if he knew how desperate I am," Josephine said. "I won't mind sleeping in the barn and doing all the chores."

"Your stepmother will not have you," Aunt Lena said. She walked over to a small desk, opened a drawer, and took out a letter. "Before you have romantic fantasies about going home, Josephine, you would do well to read and ponder this letter. Your father sent it to me before you left home. He had the minister write it for him."

Josephine took the letter and read it by the flickering kerosene lamp.

Dear Lena:

I am begging your help in a matter that troubles me deeply. My wife insists that Josephine leave this farm before another fall comes. In spite of all my hopes and efforts,

Lillian has never had warm feelings for my children from dear Madeline. My son, John, left as early as he could and is now out West. But Josephine remains a thorn in Lillian's side. Lillian will make my life miserable until Josephine is gone from here. If you could find her a job in one of the mills, I would be very grateful.

Your brother-in-law,
Amos Thorpe

Aunt Lena took the letter back from Josephine's trembling hands and said, "I have always been a friend of Mr. Fergus who owns the mill. He was kind enough to offer you a job. And now, how have you repaid him? You took part in a vicious brawl at the mill. You have humiliated me in Mr. Fergus's eyes. My own niece . . . the girl he made a place for in spite of the bad economic times . . ."

"My father would take me back if he knew I had no other place to go," Josephine insisted. She still clung to that hope, even after reading the letter.

"His marriage to Lillian means everything in the world to him," Aunt Lena said. "He will not sacrifice his wife for you. A man will never give up his wife for the sake of a child. That is not in the nature of a man."

Josephine put her head down and wept.

"You may cry all you want, but nothing will be changed," Aunt Lena said. "You *ought* to weep oceans of bitter tears of sorrow over your misdeeds. Tomorrow I will beg Mr. Fergus to find a new job for you. He will never allow you back in the mill. You are blacklisted at that job. But Mr. Fergus may have need of a servant in his home. You can scrub his floors on your knees as you repent your errors."

Josephine wished she were dead. She would not have minded in the least if her heart stopped before she drew another breath.

8 Josephine lay down on the mat in the corner of the kitchen and pulled the blanket over her. She heard Aunt Lena going upstairs to her bedroom. Then the house fell silent.

Tears streamed down Josephine's face. She couldn't lie on her back. Her whole backside was hot and raw from Aunt Lena's violent blows. Josephine couldn't bear to think about tomorrow. Of Aunt Lena dragging her to the Fergus house to be a slave to that rich family. Aunt Lena would surely send a letter to Josephine's father, too, describing her fall from grace. How she had been fired from the mill and now worked as a servant. No doubt Josephine's father would send Josephine a sorrowful letter detailing his disappointment. Josephine's entire future looked bleak beyond belief.

Josephine suddenly sat up on the floor. The stairs creaked as someone came downstairs. Josephine stared into the darkness as a figure materialized before her eyes. "Prudie!" Josephine whispered. "What are you doing down here?"

"Oh, Jo, I'm sorry I got you involved in all of this. I swear I never wanted to get you in trouble. You're the only true friend I've ever had," Prudence said quietly. She knelt down on the floor beside Josephine.

"Prudie, tomorrow Aunt Lena is taking me to the Fergus house to be a servant," Josephine said, still choking on her tears.

"The old devil," Prudence muttered darkly. "Well, won't she be surprised to find us both gone."

"Gone? What are you saying, Prudie?" Josephine asked.

Josephine saw then that Prudence carried the two carpetbags that Josephine had brought from the farm. "I've packed all of your stuff, Jo. I packed mine too. I even took your doll from the bed and packed her too," Prudence said. "I put my carpetbag outside already. You and I are going to Boston, Jo. And let the devil take them all here, for all we care," Prudence said.

"Prudie, I can't! I mean, how can we do it? I only have two dollars, surely not enough to make a trip to Boston. Prudie, I've got to do what Aunt Lena wants.

Though I hate the thought of it," Josephine said.

"Jo, you said you wanted your life to make a difference. If you get shut up in the Fergus house, your life will be hopeless drudgery. You'll be working your fingers to the bone and running and doing for them day and night. Before you know it, you'll be an old crone yourself with your whole life behind you," Prudence said.

"Prudie," Josephine cried, "I'm just 14 years old. I can't strike out on my own!"

"I'll be with you, Jo. I've got some money saved." Prudence grabbed Josephine's shoulders, causing her to wince briefly. "You won't be on your own. We'll be together. We can do anything if we stick together. We'll get a room in Boston and get good jobs." Prudence said.

"B-but how will we get to Boston?" Josephine asked.

"It's only about 20 miles. Orville will take us in his wagon," Prudence said.

"That drunk?" Josephine gasped.

"Oh, he's all right. He's just a 'Weary Willie.' He's a poor soldier who's lost his way. But he has a good heart. I could tell that right away," Prudence said.

"I don't know," Josephine answered. "I'm not sure what to do."

"We must go right now, Jo. If your aunt wakes up and finds us, she'll beat you senseless and maybe kill me. Come on now, hurry up and get dressed," Prudence said. Prudence stood in the doorway, watching for Aunt Lena to come down the stairs.

Josephine dressed, all the time telling herself it was crazy to run away to Boston with Prudence Kinney. And yet, how could she stay here? How could she be a servant girl in the house of that cruel old man who owned the mill? All the work of the house would be on her head. She'd have to clean and cook. Twenty-four hours a day she'd be at their beck and call.

A servant's wages were so low, Josephine feared she would never save enough money to go to school and be somebody. She would never even learn to compose a good letter. Like her father, she would have to dictate her thoughts to a minister or a lawyer in order to sound intelligent.

Besides, now Josephine had nobody who truly cared about her except Prudence Kinney. It would have been easy for Prudence to just leave alone. But she wanted to take Josephine with her. Prudence cared about Josephine. She was a friend, even better than Addie. So finally, though trembling with fear, Josephine followed Prudence out into the darkness. She clutched a carpetbag in each hand, and her legs wobbled with terror.

The two girls snuck through the darkness and finally reached the old wagon where Orville slept. Prudence shook him awake. "Orville, you must help us. We need to get to Boston."

"Whaaa—?" the young man mumbled.

"It's me, Prudie. Do you remember when you said you liked me and would do anything in the world for me? Well, my friend and I must get to Boston right away," Prudence said.

Orville scratched his head and slowly crawled from his blanket. Josephine observed that he had slept off most of the whiskey. Because of this, he didn't seem to remember promising Prudence anything.

"You'd really help us out . . ." Prudence continued. "You're the only hope we have." Josephine swallowed hard. What if Orville said no? She didn't want to think about returning to the boardinghouse to face Aunt Lena. About reporting to Mr. Slattery's house. About becoming his slave. Orville just had to take them to Boston!

"Well . . . I guess I could," Orville said hesitantly.

"Oh, thank you Orville!" Prudence cried. "You're our hero!"

"Hero . . . yeah . . . I could be a hero again," Orville mumbled. He seemed to be deep in thought. "Like when I was in the Army of the Ohio. It was April. General Buell ordered us to meet General Grant's forces at Shiloh. We counterattacked the Confederates. We drove those Johnny Rebs all the way to Mississippi."

"Sounds exciting," Josephine said. She remembered learning about the Battle of Shiloh. She knew that a lot of men died. Maybe that was why Orville became a "Weary Willy."

"Yeah, exciting . . ." Orville continued. "The Confederates lost 13,000 men. But we lost 30,000. Saw my friends die right beside me . . ."

"But you helped save the Union. You helped win the war," Josephine said. "You ought to be proud of that."

Orville's face lit up. "Yeah, you're right. And now I can be a hero again. This time to two pretty girls," he said, putting his hat atop his head. Josephine and Prudence blushed. "I'll take you to Boston. I just hope the wagon doesn't smell too bad. The wind might have carried some of the garbage odor away."

"No, it's fine, Orville," Prudence reassured, climbing into the wagon. But she and Josephine had to hold their breaths while Orville wasn't looking. The stench from the refuse still lingered.

"We've never been to Boston," Prudence told Orville as the wagon rolled. "Have you?"

Orville smiled and nodded. He was a handsome young man and as good-natured as anybody would want. Too bad he wasn't really rich, Josephine thought.

But then the nice ones seldom are. "Yeah, I've been to Boston. It's a bustlin' town. Lotta Irish immigrants there. Hundreds and thousands of 'em I guess."

Josephine remembered what the vegetable vendor had said about the Irish immigrants. She became worried that they wouldn't be able to find jobs.

"Are there a lot of jobs there?" Josephine asked.

"Lotta jobs, and plenty askin' for 'em too," Orville said.

Josephine turned to Prudence. "What if we don't find work?"

"We will," Prudence said. "There's always work for young people with energy."

"The Irish are crowded in tenements. Like nothin' you ever saw. A hundred people living in a three-decker house where maybe a dozen ought to be. They do piecework, sewing for the factories. Whole family works, even the little ones," Orville said.

"It must be dreadful," Josephine said.

When the wagon rolled into the outskirts of Boston, daybreak had already come. Everywhere there were people hurrying about. Josephine stared in awe at the crowded streets, the buildings, the hustle and bustle of the people. She had never seen so many people in one place before.

Orville dropped the girls off in a poor neighborhood in the north end of Boston. He tipped his hat at the girls. "Good luck to you," he said.

Josephine felt scared as Orville drove away in his wagon. Although she barely knew him, she had somehow felt safe with him. At least he was somewhat familiar. Here she saw nothing like she had ever seen before. The three-story buildings faced narrow streets. Many gaudy saloons vied for business. She felt so alone. But Prudence interrupted her thoughts.

"It all looks strange and scary now, but we'll be fine," Prudence said with a brave smile.

A woman with a young girl at her side carried a load of garments on her head. She was walking toward one of the tenements.

"Are there rooms there?" Prudence asked her.

The woman nodded, and Josephine and Prudence followed her through a door where all the paint had peeled off. Prudence found a middle-aged woman in a downstairs room. The woman offered them a room in the cellar for four dollars a month.

"Will you take a dollar now and the rest later?" Prudence asked. The woman nodded, and Prudence fished a dollar from her bag. In a few minutes the girls were heading downstairs into the cellar. Josephine got kind of excited at the thought of their own place.

Their room was at the end of a dark passageway. "Oh," Josephine groaned when she saw the room illuminated by an oil lamp. The room contained one bed, a cooking stove, and two wooden chairs.

Josephine didn't even want to put her bags down in this dirty, awful place. It was the filthiest place she had ever seen. After showing them how the stove worked, the lady left and closed the splintering door. Finally Josephine's arms ached so much from carrying the carpetbags that she gave in and put them down. "Prudie, how can we live here?" Josephine asked.

"We can for a little while. When we save some money, we can move up in the world, Jo," Prudence said cheerfully. Josephine wasn't sure how Prudence could keep her spirits up. But if Prudence could do it, Josephine figured she could at least try.

Josephine walked around the room, trying not to touch anything.

"But before we can save any money, we need to find some jobs," Prudence said.

Josephine sighed at the thought of looking for work. Aunt Lena had arranged her job in Baldwin. And look how that had turned out. Josephine dreaded the thought of having to find work herself in some awful place.

"Quit thinkin' those bad thoughts and come on," Prudence said as she pulled Josephine toward the door.

The two girls began walking down the crowded, dirty street. The throng of people was like a current, pushing the girls along. They stopped in every store and every factory asking if anybody was hiring sewing machine girls. Most of the factories were already full and not in need of any workers. Josephine could see many young children working alongside their mothers in the dark sweatshops. She thought once again about what the vegetable vendor had said and began to get very discouraged. By late afternoon, Josephine was so tired she thought her legs would collapse under her.

Despair clawed at Josephine like a slimy sea monster under the water when you cannot swim anymore. Josephine wished that she had died with her mother. That would have been better, she thought. There was no one left to care about her or to care for her, so she should have died too. Josephine believed in heaven, and she wished she were in heaven now with her mother. She wished she were anywhere but on this mob-filled, filthy street in Boston.

"Jo!" Prudence cried as she came running out of a grimy storefront. "They have work in there for us! For both of us! We get paid for every pair of pants we finish. If we're very fast, we can make more money than we did in Baldwin. It's a garment factory, and a lot of girls work in there."

"But it's so small," Josephine said, sizing up the store.

"Yes. But there are a lot of sewing machines. We're going to be all right, Jo. We start tomorrow, first thing. Let's go and get something to eat now. There are a lot of little restaurants. Look—Harry's Place. Let's go in there. I'm hungry as a horse, Jo," Prudence said.

Josephine and Prudence went into Harry's Place and sat down to large steaming bowls of beef stew and fresh bread. Josephine hadn't eaten since noon the day before. She had been so frightened and miserable that she couldn't eat. Now hunger pains took over, and she wolfed down the food.

"Dip the bread in the stew, Jo. It tastes so delicious," Prudence advised. "Everything in the world looks better when your stomach is full."

A ghost of a smile tugged at Josephine's mouth. "Are you sure they're hiring us at that garment factory, Prudie?" Josephine asked. "You're not just saying that to cheer me, are you?"

"No. We start in the morning. The man in charge seems like an ignorant fool, but he's not as bad as Slattery. I think we'll be all right. He said if we want, we can take work home too and make more money that way. We can take pants home and overcast the seams in our room. And then we can take them back in the morning," Prudence said.

Josephine was feeling a mix of emotions. Relief. Fear. Fatigue. A tear slipped from her eye, and Prudence caught a glimpse of it as she looked up from her soup.

Prudence stopped eating and frowned at Josephine. "Now what's the matter?" Prudence asked. "Honestly, Jo, we've been through so much. Now we're finally coming out of the woods, and you have to start bawling on me!"

9 A smile flickered on Josephine's face. "I cry sometimes when things look better, Prudie. I just felt so hopeless, but now I'm starting to feel better," she said. Her life was beginning to look more auspicious.

In the morning Josephine and Prudence went to the garment factory. It was just a large room packed with sewing machines and workers. Josephine could barely get through the narrow aisle to her machine. It was much worse than the Baldwin mill. Debris was piled everywhere. And if there were ever a fire, there would be a deadly stampede to the single door. Here they not only smelled the oil lamps but also the stench of the garbage piled up in the alley. Josephine grew so sick she thought she might vomit.

Josephine tackled the stack of men's trousers, sewing the pieces together quickly. She was experienced now. Working in Baldwin had done that much for her.

A young man with a bald spot atop his head ran from worker to worker, giving advice on how to do the work more quickly. "It's all in eliminating motions . . . the fewer the motions, the more quickly you go," he said. He wasn't vicious like Mr. Slattery. He was more annoying. Like a fly that will not stop circling your head no matter how many times you brush it away.

Josephine worked hard all day and earned only $1.50. But she was determined that tomorrow she would be faster.

"Do you want homework?" the boss asked as the girls were getting up from their machines.

Prudence and Josephine looked at each other. They were both so enervated that they could not imagine working more tonight. All they wanted to do was get to that horrid little room and go to sleep. But how far would $1.50 take them?

"Yes, I'll take some home," Josephine said.

"Good, we need buttons on all these shirts," the boss said. He piled the work in Josephine's arms.

Prudence was taking homework too. She was finding it hard to carry until an Irish girl came over.

"If you carry the clothes atop your

head, it's easy," the rosy-cheeked girl said. She looked robust, as if the long hours in the sweatshop had not yet sapped her health. She gathered the clothes in a compact bundle and piled it atop Josephine's head. Then she did the same for Prudence. "Just balance it with one hand, and off you go," she said.

When the two girls reached the little room, they made a pile of the shirts. Josephine lit the kerosene lamp. They just wanted to get some sleep, but they made themselves stay up. Each sat on one of the old chairs, sewing buttons on the shirts.

"It's so dark in here," Josephine said.

"Come closer to the lamp, Jo," Prudence said. "Come on, let's hurry and sew the buttons on. We get a penny a shirt. If we can finish all these shirts, then we get another 50 cents."

The girls worked until 11:00 before they finished. Then they crawled into bed. Josephine dug her doll from the carpetbag and clutched it to her chest all night. It made her mother seem very close to her. Close enough to talk to, as Josephine sometimes did.

"Ma," Josephine whispered in the darkness, "can you see me from where you are? I'm a sad case now, Ma. I miss you so much. I miss how you loved me. Now nobody loves me. Except maybe Prudie. But there never will be anyone who loves me like you did, Ma."

Josephine looked over at Prudence who was already fast asleep. It didn't take Josephine long to follow her friend into the world of dreams.

* * *

The only day off from the factory was Sunday. Early Sunday morning, Josephine wrote a letter home.

Dear Father,
    I guess by now you know I'm not at Aunt Lena's. I'm sure Aunt Lena has told you how wicked I am. But it did not happen like she said. The boss at the mill was evil. I will never go back to Aunt Lena's. I almost hate her now, though I know hating is a sin. I am in the north

end of Boston with my friend. We
live in a dirty room and work in a
garment factory. My life is hard
and bitter. I know I can never come
home. I will not bother you. I just
wanted to tell my side of what
happened and to give you my
address if you ever want to write.

Your daughter,
Josephine

"Jo," Prudence said, "let's go see the
rest of Boston."

Josephine was tired. But the thought of
spending Sunday in this dirty room was
enough to make her agree. Although
Josephine's legs ached from being
cramped under the sewing machine, she
joined Prudence. They boarded the
streetcar for the ride to Boston Common.

There were about 50 people on the
streetcar, and the mules pulled it slowly
along. The smell of so many people
packed together on a warm day made
Josephine sick. It reminded her of the
factory. She was glad to finally get off the
streetcar into the fresh air.

"Look at that beautiful green grass!" Prudence shouted when they reached the Common.

"Oh, Prudie," Josephine cried, "I haven't seen anything so lovely since I last saw a farm meadow!"

"And look at the trees," Prudence said. "Oh, Jo, let's sit awhile under the trees and eat our sandwiches. The grass smells so sweet. And I hear birds singing. Oh, my, I'd forgotten the sound of birdsong." Prudence lay back on the grass and stared at the cloudless sky. "Someday I'll have a fine house with grass in front. And birds will be singing in *my* trees."

Josephine's mind returned to her childhood. When she was about five and her brother, John, was 13, he made her a rope swing and hung it from an oak tree. On one particular day he spent all afternoon pushing Josephine higher and higher on the swing. It was as if she would eventually fly right among the clouds. With so many years between Josephine and her brother, they weren't together often. But occasionally John would take time from his friends to be a big brother to Josephine. And those times were special.

John remained at the farm for about six months after their mother died. Then Father began courting Lillian. John didn't like Lillian any more than Josephine did, but he could do something about it. He was a big, strapping 18-year-old boy. He wasn't a scared little ten-year-old.

"Sis, I'm goin'," John told Josephine one rainy night. The wind howled and the rain came down in great silvery sheets.

"You're not going *now*, are you?" Josephine had asked.

"Yeah, I am. I'm goin' west to Colorado. Jeremy and I are goin' together. Lotta silver out there, and we're gettin' our fair share. We're goin' to Leadville and gettin' rich. And then I'll come back for you," John had said.

But he never came back for her.

Maybe there was no silver in Leadville after all.

Josephine would never forget the last time she saw her brother. He hugged her, and then he walked off into the silvery rain. In some strange way, he seemed to turn into silver himself before he vanished.

"What're you thinking about, Jo?" Prudence asked.

"My brother, John. I was wondering whatever happened to him," Josephine said.

Prudence shrugged. "If he's anything like my brothers, you'll never see hide nor hair of him. I have two older brothers, and when Pa wasn't beatin' on me, they were. My grandma was the only one who cared about me. She had a saying, 'you pick your friends, but you get stuck with kin.' That's the truth. If I coulda picked, I never would've been born in my family."

The girls ate lunch at a little restaurant near Boston Common. Then toward evening, they caught the streetcar home.

As they walked from the streetcar to their building, they heard the familiar sounds they were becoming so accustomed to. Night and day the sounds of children crying and coughing could be heard. There was a lot of sickness in the tenement. And it wasn't unusual when someone died, most often a small child or baby. Josephine felt so sorry for the children. At least she had had a happy childhood until she was ten. But for these impoverished children, there was nothing but hard work and little to eat. An occasional orange or small piece of cake and their little faces would light up with joy. So sometimes Josephine bought a few oranges and passed them out to the children in the tenement.

"Jo," Prudence scolded, "you're as bad off as they are. Save your money for your own self!"

But Josephine continued to buy oranges for the children.

The work at the garment factory became deadly dull. Josephine was put on one task—making sleeves for men's shirts. She kept repeating the same tedious motions, over and over, a hundred times a day. Her arms ached from overuse of the same muscles. Sometimes her arms felt so heavy that she could barely lift them. Josephine felt as if she herself had become amalgamated with the whirring machine. She didn't feel like a human being anymore. Yet the machine did not ache as she did. And the machine didn't weep with weariness.

Josephine and Prudence had been very frugal with their wages. But at the end of the first month in Boston, Josephine counted the money she had saved—two dollars. Everything else had gone for food and rent.

"Prudie, we'll never escape this life," Josephine groaned.

"Yes, we will. We're getting better and better at our work. The homework is paying more now. You'll see, Jo. Don't get down. Listen, I bought some chicken for us tonight. I'll fry it good and brown, and we'll have a feast," Prudence said.

Soon the tiny room smelled almost good with frying chicken. A smile danced on Josephine's lips. "Oh, that does smell good!"

Prudence laughed. "After we stuff ourselves with chicken, we'll feel new again. Don't fret, Jo, the sun will shine on us again someday . . . . I just know it . . . . Someday the sun will shine again . . . ."

10 Josephine began noticing a difference in herself when she looked in the mirror. The round little girl's face framed by red braids was gone. Josephine had never been able to see her cheekbones, but now she could. And her complexion was sallow from spending endless hours indoors. She stared into the cracked little mirror by the light of the lamp. "Prudie, I'm growing old. I look haggard," she said.

"No, you're gettin' a woman's face. You're not that pudgy-faced little girl you were when we first met. You're much prettier now, Jo. You should be glad of that," Prudence said.

"I'll be 15 on Sunday," Josephine said.

"*This* Sunday?" Prudence asked. "Then we have to celebrate!"

"Don't be silly, Prudie. We don't have money to celebrate. And besides, what's there to celebrate?" Josephine grumbled. She glanced around at their abject living conditions.

Josephine's father had not written back to her. Aunt Lena had probably poisoned her father against her completely, she thought. He most likely wanted nothing more to do with her.

Josephine wept on the night before her birthday. She was extra tired from sewing buttons on tons of shirts. She clutched her doll and finally fell into an exhausted sleep.

In the morning Josephine felt strange. She expected to be more depressed than usual because it was her birthday, and it didn't matter to anybody. But when Prudence shook her awake and cried, "Let's celebrate, Jo!" Josephine felt a rush of excitement.

But then she took a look around their squalid room.

"Celebrate," Josephine said. "How can I?"

"Jo, listen to me. Look at all you've been through. You were thrown out of your house and worked like a slave in the mill. You've been mistreated and wronged. But you survived it. You weren't killed by it, Jo. *That's* what we'll celebrate," Prudence said.

It began to make sense to Josephine. Here in this squalor and filth and bugs, she could still smile. She was not so beaten down that she had to be sent to a madhouse. She was pale and haggard, but she was strong too. She could sew better than almost anybody else.

Yes, there was something to celebrate, she thought.

Prudence grabbed hold of Josephine, and they danced around the tiny room singing snatches of songs they'd heard.

"Cape Cod girls, they have no combs,
Comb their hair with codfish bones,
Lolly Tu Dum, Lolly Tu Dum!"

Josephine and Prudence caught the streetcar again and ended up dining on oysters and white custard sauce. Josephine bought some oranges too. And when they returned to the North End, she felt as if some great turning point had occurred in her life.

And Josephine knew what she must do.

She went to her room and lifted the doll her mother had made her from the bed. Josephine washed the doll's hair and sewed her a new little dress from bits and pieces of cloth she had brought home from the garment factory. She put a pretty pink ribbon in the doll's hair.

Then Josephine went to a downstairs apartment where a little Irish girl with huge green eyes and pink little cheeks lived.

Josephine knocked, and a small woman opened the door. She looked middle-aged, but Josephine knew she was no older than 22.

"Does your daughter have a doll?" Josephine asked.

"Oh, never," the mother said. "Dolls are so dear."

Josephine held out the doll. "This is for her."

The child, who was clinging to her mother's skirt, took the doll from her mother. She desperately hugged and kissed it.

"God bless you," the mother said when Josephine left two oranges as well. Josephine delivered the rest of the oranges to other children in the tenement.

* * *

When Josephine and Prudence got off work at the end of the following week, it was already dark. Fall was beginning to set in, making it feel like the workday was even longer. The girls were chattering about the miseries of the day when Prudence noticed they were being followed by a man.

Josephine had read lurid tales in the newspaper about young women attacked on the dark streets of Boston.

"Hurry, Prudie," Josephine whispered.

"I got a knife, Jo," Prudence said. She, too, had heard stories and swore she would be ready.

The girls hurried. But the man quickened his step too.

"Oh, God in heaven, he's gonna catch us," Josephine gasped. When they got under a street lamp, the girls spun around to face the man. Prudence wielded her knife.

"We got weapons," Prudence screamed at the man.

The young man threw back his head and laughed.

"Josie, it's me, John!" he shouted. "Pa said he got a letter from you in Boston. He said I needed to check up on you."

Josephine looked at the man under the lamplight and then leaped into her brother's arms. Prudence put her knife back.

"It's taken me a while to find you. But I knew you were somewhere in the North End. So I went to every factory until I found you," John said.

"Have you been in Colorado?" Josephine asked her brother.

"I never found silver in Colorado, Josie," John said. "But Jeremy and I have a dry goods store in Sacramento. That's in California. You wanna come back to California with me, little sister?"

Josephine turned and looked at Prudence. "Only if my friend can come too," she said.

John Thorpe laughed again and took a good look at the blond, blue-eyed friend of his sister. "Long as she doesn't stick me with that knife," he said.

Josephine and Prudence worked as salesgirls and tailors in Sacramento. Their experience in the sewing machine shops was valued, and they moved up very quickly. The girls managed to save quite a bit of money. In 1875 Prudence had saved enough to open her own seamstress shop. In 1876 Josephine went to school to learn to be a teacher.

Josephine returned to Boston in 1880 to teach and care for the poor immigrant children she had never forgotten. She also became an advocate for child labor laws. She even lived long enough to see the Fair Labor Standards Act passed in 1938. This law declared a minimum age of 18 for hazardous occupations. And it limited the number of occupations for children aged 14 and 15.

Once in a while a letter condemning unsafe labor practices would appear in the *Boston Globe* signed Josephine Thorpe. Her most famous line was, "My dream for all of the children pent up in those goods-producing dungeons is that someday the sun will shine again!"